P9-DWY-387

Franklin Endicott and the Third Key

Volume Six

Kate DiCamillo
illustrated by Chris Van Dusen

This is a work of fiction. Names, characters, places, and incidents are either products of the author's imagination or, if real, are used fictitiously.

First edition 2021

Library of Congress Catalog Card Number 2021935024
ISBN 978-1-5362-0181-9

21 22 23 24 25 26 LBM 10 9 8 7 6 5 4 3

Printed in Melrose Park, IL, USA

This book was typeset in Mrs. Eaves.
The illustrations were done in gouache.

Candlewick Press
99 Dover Street
Somerville, Massachusetts 02144

www.candlewick.com

A JUNIOR LIBRARY GUILD SELECTION

For Jane St. Anthony
K. D.

For Arthur and Evan
C. V.

FRANK
SAFETY FIRST!
RULES
NO ARMADILLOS!

Chapter One

Frank Endicott was a worrier.

He worried a lot.

He worried about leprosy (who wouldn't worry about leprosy?) and lions (they were such alarmingly violent creatures). He worried about tests (not being properly prepared for them), black holes (what happened if you got sucked into them?), and armadillos (transmitters of leprosy).

Frank worried about alligators. They looked sluggish and slow moving, but in fact, they were not slow moving at all. Alligators could move very, very quickly when they were motivated to do something—eat you, for instance.

Frank worried about submarines (getting trapped on one), brown recluse spiders (being bitten by one), vampire bats (carriers of rabies), and rabies (which could kill you).

Also, Frank worried about goats.

There was no good reason to worry about goats, but Frank worried about them nonetheless—their eyes were so unnerving and otherworldly.

Frank had so many things that he worried about that he kept a notebook exclusively for his worries. He listed the worries alphabetically. He indexed them and cross-referenced them.

He felt that his worries were legitimate—fact based and solidly researched (except, perhaps, for the goat worry)—but Frank was embarrassed by how many worries he had.

Were his worries out of control?

Was his worrying excessive?

It worried him to think so.

Frank had a little sister named Stella, and (he couldn't help it) it worried him to think that Stella would discover his notebook and read the gruesome facts recorded within its pages and become a worrier herself.

And so, Frank started hiding the worry notebook under his bed.

And that's when the nightmares began.

They were terrifying—filled with goat eyes and speedy alligators and vicious lions and all-consuming black holes. And also, armadillos.

Sometimes, the dreams were so terrible (being stuck on a submarine with an armadillo, for instance) that Frank woke up screaming, and Stella had to come into his room and kneel by his bed and hold his hand and tell him that everything was going to be fine, that he was safe.

Frank appreciated her kindness very much, but he was also somewhat dismayed by it. He was the big brother, after all; he should be comforting her.

After several nights of nightmares, Frank took the notebook out from underneath the bed. He moved it downstairs

to the hall closet. He put it on the top shelf.

The nightmares, alas, continued.

Frank decided something had to change.

And so one day after school, Frank went over to the Lincoln sisters' house and knocked on the door.

Eugenia Lincoln answered. She looked slightly annoyed. But then, Eugenia Lincoln always looked slightly annoyed. Frank was used to it.

"Yes, Franklin?" she said.

"Good afternoon, Miss Lincoln," said Frank. "I was wondering if I might use your encyclopedias to do a bit of research."

"Certainly," said Eugenia, who approved of research. "I extend you carte blanche." She held the door open wide.

"Thank you," said Frank. He went into the Lincoln sisters' living room and stood before the Bingham Lincoln Encyclopedia set. The books had been written by the Lincoln sisters' grandfather, Bingham Lincoln, and they were very old. The entries were dense and comprehensive and featured many colorful and instructive illustrations. Reading one entry naturally led to another entry and then another volume, and a slowly burgeoning belief that the world was an orderly, reasonable place—a belief that Frank very much wanted to subscribe to.

"Make sure you return everything to its rightful place," said Eugenia Lincoln.

"Yes, Miss Lincoln," said Frank.

Baby Lincoln stuck her head into the living room. She said, "Hello, Franklin. Grandfather Lincoln would be so happy to see how you appreciate his encyclopedias."

"Franklin is engaged in research, Baby," said Eugenia. "Do not disturb him."

"Yes, Sister," said Baby. Baby always agreed with Eugenia. Or at least she pretended to.

Baby Lincoln and Eugenia Lincoln disappeared, and Frank settled in with the encyclopedias. He followed the "nightmare" entry to the "ancient myth" entry. He read about night witches and demons and goblins and trolls. He read that in some cultures, there were mythical creatures that actually consumed nightmares. Wouldn't it be

wonderful to have someone sit at the foot of your bed and eat your nightmares?

But where could Frank find a creature bold enough to face his nightmares and hungry enough to devour them?

Suddenly, Frank had an idea — a marvelous idea, a comforting idea.

He closed the encyclopedia with a decisive *thump*. He gathered up his notebook and his pencils and pens.

"Thank you very much," he called out to the Lincoln sisters.

"I hope you returned everything to its rightful place," Eugenia shouted back.

"Come again," said Baby.

Frank left the Lincolns' house and went down the street and knocked on the Watsons' door.

Mrs. Watson answered. "Frank," she said. "How lovely to see you."

"Hello, Mrs. Watson," said Frank. "I have a somewhat unusual request."

Chapter Two

"Yay, yay!" said Stella. "It's a slumber party with a pig. I want to sleep in here, too!"

"It's not a slumber party with a pig," said Frank. "It's a scientific experiment. I will keep you posted as to its efficacy. In the meantime, I will have to request that you sleep in your own room."

"Shoot," said Stella. "I never get to have any fun." She turned and left Frank's room very slowly.

"Now," said Frank. He looked at Mercy. He stared into the pig's eyes. He said, "I need you to stay awake. I need you to consume my nightmares. Do you understand?"

Mercy stared back at him. She blinked.

Frank wasn't sure that she comprehended what was expected of her. It was hard to tell what pigs were thinking. Their eyes were so small.

Frank got into bed. He said, "Stay right there, Mercy. Stay vigilant and true."

The pig snorted.

Frank turned off the light.

"Okay," he said to the darkness and to the pig, "here we go."

Frank dreamed about a flying alligator. The alligator's wings were constructed from old umbrellas, and in the dream, the alligator hovered above Frank smiling a toothy, terrifying smile. The dream was suffused with an air of impending doom.

Frank woke with a jolt. His heart was thumping loudly. He was sweating. Mercy had taken over most of the bed and pushed Frank to the very edge.

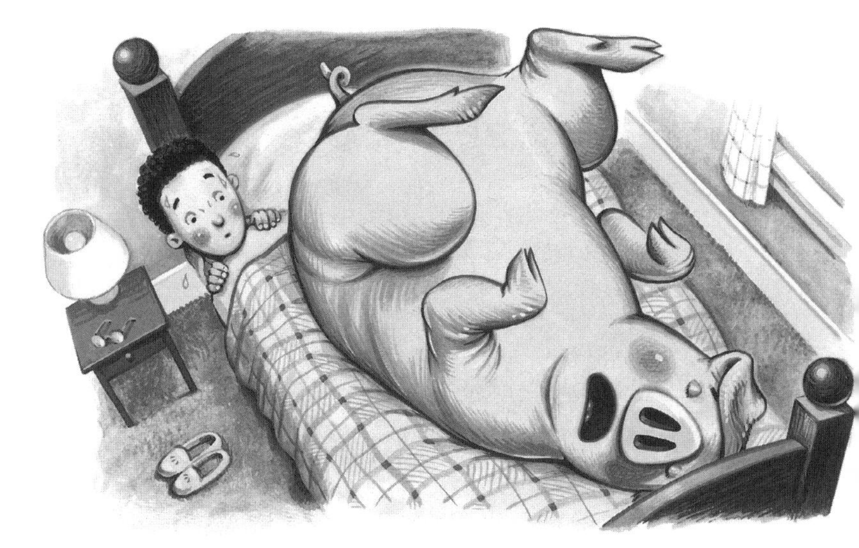

The pig was snoring loudly. She had protected him from nothing.

Frank stared up at the ceiling. What if Mercy rolled over in her sleep and crushed him? He sighed. What a ridiculous worry. But still, he got up, went downstairs, and heated some milk in a saucepan. According to the Bingham Lincoln Encyclopedia, warm milk was an effective sleep aid.

Frank looked out the window and saw that the Lincolns' kitchen light was on. He could see Eugenia Lincoln's profile. She looked annoyed.

Frank added more milk to the saucepan. He got a piece of paper from his notebook and wrote a note to his parents and Stella: *Dear Family, if you wake and find me gone, do not worry. I have simply journeyed next door to visit Eugenia Lincoln. I will, of course, return. Yours, Frank.* He put the note on the kitchen table.

When the milk was sufficiently warm, Frank added some honey and a little cinnamon, poured the milk into two mugs, and went out the back door and across the yard to the Lincoln sisters' house.

He knocked on the side door. He called out, "Miss Lincoln? I had a terrible nightmare. I've brought you some warm milk. Can I come inside?"

Frank and Eugenia sat together at the kitchen table. Frank told Eugenia about his worry notebook, and how placing it under his bed had led to some unfortunate and very disturbing nightmares, the most recent of which had featured an alligator who had fashioned wings from an umbrella.

"Ludicrous," said Eugenia Lincoln. "Absurd. Alligators don't have wings. And since they don't have opposable thumbs, they are incapable of *constructing* wings. Furthermore, you are afraid of too many things, Franklin."

"Yes, Miss Lincoln," said Frank.

There was something oddly comforting about Eugenia's brusqueness, her cavalier dismissal of his nightmare, and her annoyed insistence that he was too afraid of too many things.

Frank said, "Are you often awake in the middle of the night, Miss Lincoln?"

"That is entirely too personal a question," said Eugenia. She took a sip of her warm milk. She sighed. She said, "Yes, I am often awake in the middle

of the night. I am a lifelong sufferer of insomnia."

"I've read about insomnia," said Frank.

"Yes, well, reading about insomnia is one thing. Suffering it is another."

"Yes, Miss Lincoln," said Frank.

A silence descended. Frank noticed that there was a single key in the center of the kitchen table.

"What's the key for, Miss Lincoln?" he said.

"The key needs to be duplicated," said Eugenia. "That's tomorrow's task—one of tomorrow's tasks. When you can't sleep, the best thing to do is to concentrate on life's daily tasks, to attend to the mundane. Tomorrow, I will attend to my business. I will go and get the key duplicated."

Attending to the mundane struck Frank as a very comforting notion.

"Can I go with you?" said Frank. "Can I help you attend to your daily tasks?"

"I suppose you may," said Eugenia.

"Thank you, Miss Lincoln," said Frank. He got up from the table and returned home. He could hear Mercy snoring as soon as he entered the house.

He went upstairs and walked down the hallway and looked in Stella's room and saw that Mercy was in Stella's bed.

Stella was smiling. She had her arm draped over the leg of the pig.

Frank got back in bed. He pulled the covers up to his chin. He closed his eyes and saw the key sitting on the kitchen table.

"Attend to the mundane," he said to himself. "Do your daily tasks."

And with the key glowing brightly in his mind, Frank Endicott fell asleep.

Chapter Three

The next day, Frank went downtown with Eugenia Lincoln.

"Here we are," said Eugenia. She stopped in front of a store called Buddy Lamp's Used Goods. There was a small sign propped in the plate glass window. The sign said KEYS MADE, SAWS SHARPENED, MYSTERIES CONSIDERED, USED ITEMS BOUGHT AND SOLD.

Did the considering of mysteries a
the making of keys really belong in the same sentence?

Frank didn't think so.

"Shouldn't we go to a hardware store for key duplication?" said Frank.

"I use Buddy Lamp," said Eugenia. "I have always used Buddy Lamp, and I will continue to use Buddy Lamp."

"Yes, Miss Lincoln," said Frank.

"I am very set in my ways," said Eugenia Lincoln. "And Buddy Lamp is utterly reliable."

"If you say so," said Frank. He stared at the window display for Buddy Lamp's Used Goods. It featured a mannequin wearing a green suit. The mannequin had no head; furthermore, a dead weasel

was sitting on the headless mannequin's right shoulder. The weasel's lips were pulled back in a snarl, revealing very sharp weasel teeth.

Frank took a step backward. He wished that he had his notebook with him. He felt a strong urge to make an entry, to write down the words *weasel teeth.*

"Maybe I'll just wait in the car, Miss Lincoln," said Frank.

"You will not wait in the car, Franklin Endicott," said Eugenia. "You will step forward bravely. That is what you will do." She opened the door to Buddy Lamp's. A cluster of sleigh bells affixed to the door handle jingled in a merry, heedless way. "After you," said Eugenia Lincoln.

KEYS MADE,
SAWS
SHARPENED,
MYSTERIES
CONSIDERED,
USED ITEMS
BOUGHT AND SOLD

Frank stepped into the dark interior of Buddy Lamp's Used Goods. He immediately bumped into somebody.

"Pardon me," said Frank.

He turned and found himself face-to-face with Napoleon Bonaparte, a man who appeared quite often in the Bingham Lincoln Encyclopedia set.

"Aaack," said Frank.

"Ah," said a voice, "he is, indeed, quite lifelike. Isn't he? He hails from a first-rate, but now defunct, wax museum in Toledo, Ohio. I am quite pleased to have procured him."

"Good afternoon, Mr. Lamp," said Eugenia.

A man slowly emerged from the gloom. He was very tall. His hair was gray. He

looked like someone made from a piece of paper that had been folded over and over again until it was creased and worn.

"Good afternoon to you, Miss Lincoln. I see that you've brought a friend." The man bowed in Frank's direction.

Frank, uncertain of the proper protocol, bowed back.

"Mr. Lamp," said Eugenia. "I would like to introduce you to my good friend and neighbor, Franklin Endicott."

"It's a pleasure to make your acquaintance," said Buddy Lamp.

"I have come to have a duplicate key made," said Eugenia. She held out the key to Buddy Lamp, who took it from her and bowed again.

"I have several other errands to attend to," said Eugenia. "Franklin, I will have you wait here and procure the keys."

"Wait here?" said Frank. His voice squeaked in alarm. It was so dark in the store, and Buddy Lamp was so odd. Also,

Frank felt as if Napoleon Bonaparte were staring right at him. He could feel other things waiting in the shadows — strange things, worrisome things, things that should probably be recorded and indexed in the worry notebook.

"I will return shortly," said Eugenia Lincoln.

She pushed open the door of Buddy Lamp's Used Goods. The sleigh bells emitted their festive jingle.

"Humdee dum dee," said Buddy Lamp. "I will get busy on this key immediately, young Mr. Endicott. In the meantime, if you would like to peruse what is on offer here in the store, I extend you a hearty welcome to do just that. Let your curiosity be piqued. Allow yourself the freedom to explore, to question, to revel in life's myriad mysteries!"

"Okay," said Frank, even though he wasn't all that fond of reveling in mysteries.

Buddy Lamp went behind the counter. Soon, there was the soft whir of a machine, the busy sound of something being made.

Frank stood in the gloom. Truly, he felt a little reluctant to move. Who knew what other wax-figure emperors were waiting to leap out at him?

But deep within the store, Frank saw something glinting, beckoning.

He took a step forward, and then another step.

And soon, Franklin Endicott was swallowed by the shadows.

Chapter Four

It turned out that the shelves of Buddy Lamp's Used Goods were stocked with an amazing assortment of things.

The first item that Frank picked up—the glinting thing that had beckoned him farther into the store—was a large chunk of amber. It was beautiful. Frank held it up to the dim light and saw that inside the golden amber some long-dead insect was suspended, trapped for all eternity.

ROBOTS OF THE WORLD
PUZZLE

Wouldn't it be terrible to be stuck for all eternity inside a piece of amber?

Frank shivered.

He carefully put the amber (and its doomed insect) back on the shelf.

He picked up a magic set. The edges of the box were frayed and held together with yellowed tape.

SWEETLAND'S MAGIC SET. BECOME THE NEXT HOUDINI IF YOU DARE. AMAZE YOUR FRIENDS! PUNISH YOUR ENEMIES! MAKE THINGS APPEAR AND DISAPPEAR AT WILL!

Frank shook the box. Something inside of it rattled in a forlorn way.

Frank had read a great deal about the magician Harry Houdini. Houdini had been able to pick locks and break chains and hold his breath for an incredibly long time. Frank doubted very seriously that the Sweetland's Magic Set held the necessary materials for a person to become the next Houdini.

He returned the box to the shelf without even looking inside, and then he stood with his hands behind his back and considered a jar that seemed to be

filled with eyeballs. But that couldn't be, could it? How could you put eyeballs in a jar? *Who* would put eyeballs in a jar?

Next to the eyeball jar, there was a stovepipe hat, the kind of hat that Abraham Lincoln would have worn.

The store had grown suddenly quiet. The whir of the key-making machine had been silenced.

Frank looked up.

"Eeep," he said. He jumped a small jump.

Buddy Lamp had soundlessly materialized out of nowhere to stand beside Frank.

"I see you are admiring the stovepipe hat," said Buddy Lamp. "I'm happy to inform you that yes, indeed, it does date from the time of Abraham Lincoln.

As to whether Mr. Lincoln wore this particular hat—well, that is a matter for some debate. I myself like to think that Mr. Lincoln *did* wear it, and that some of his wisdom and humor and kindness still reside within it."

"Abraham Lincoln was a very great man," said Frank.

"On that point, you and I are in perfect agreement."

Frank stole a glance at Buddy Lamp. The man was so insubstantial that it seemed possible he could go up in a puff of smoke at any moment.

"Humdee dum dee," said Buddy Lamp.

A profound silence descended.

The items in the gloomy store shifted and sighed.

Frank cleared his throat. He said, "I'm amazed at your selection."

"I try to aim for a certain eclecticism," said Buddy Lamp. "Many, many things interest me. Many things fascinate me. The world is filled with marvels."

"Are those eyeballs in that jar?" said Frank.

"That is exactly what they are," said Buddy Lamp. "They are not real, of course. They belong to a taxidermist. Or rather, they *did* belong to a taxidermist. Past tense, past tense. So much here involves the past tense. In any case, there are many varieties of artificial eyes in that jar—eye of leopard, eye of squirrel, eye of duck, even eye of newt, perhaps. Who knows?"

The sleigh bells on the door jingled, issuing their promise of merry and care-free days, and Eugenia Lincoln entered the store.

"Mr. Lamp," said Eugenia. "I'm assuming my duplicate key is ready."

"It is," said Buddy Lamp. He clicked his heels together. "Just one moment, please."

Buddy Lamp went behind the counter and came back with a brown envelope. "Here you are," he said. "I'm pleased to have been of service." He handed the envelope to Frank.

Buddy Lamp bowed at Eugenia, and then he bowed at Frank. He said, "I hope to see you both again soon."

Frank thought it was unlikely that he would ever return to Buddy Lamp's Used Goods. The store was entirely too disturbing.

Nonetheless, Frank bowed back at Buddy Lamp. He thanked him.

It wasn't until Eugenia Lincoln turned the car onto Deckawoo Drive that Frank thought to look inside the envelope.

"Uh-oh," said Frank.

"What now?" said Eugenia.

"There are three keys in here," said Frank. "And there should be only two."

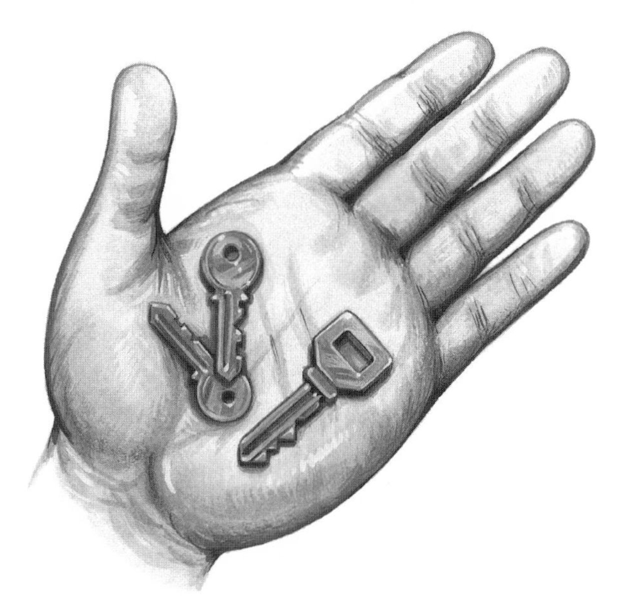

Chapter Five

The third key was not like the other two keys.

The pattern of its teeth was different. It shone in a muted, self-important way, as if it knew a secret.

"I'm sure that Buddy Lamp put the key in the envelope inadvertently," said Eugenia Lincoln. "Tomorrow, you may go and return it to him."

“But what does it mean?” said Frank.

“What does it mean?” said Eugenia. “It means that Buddy Lamp put the key in the envelope by mistake. As I said.”

Frank held the third key in his hand and stared down at it. He did not think the key was a mistake. He thought it was a message. He just didn’t know what the message was.

"I'll have to go back," he said.

"As I said," said Eugenia, "you will return the key tomorrow."

"But I'm afraid to go back there," said Frank.

"We have already discussed this, Franklin Endicott. You have entirely too many fears. Tomorrow, you will return the key to Mr. Lamp. And that's that."

He had nightmares that night. Of course he did.

He dreamed that the third key was buried in a bowl of eyeballs. He dreamed of the snarl and snap of weasel teeth. He dreamed that the headless mannequin in the green suit could speak—in spite of the fact that it didn't have a head.

"Give me back my key!" the headless mannequin shouted.

Frank woke with a start. He got up, turned on the light, and went downstairs. He got the worry notebook out of the hall closet. He made several entries: eyeballs (fake), bugs in amber (for all eternity), weasels (their teeth), headless men (talking), and keys (of unexplained origin).

And then he returned the notebook to the top shelf and went into the kitchen and heated up some milk. He looked out the window. The Lincoln sisters' light was not on. Eugenia was not sitting at the kitchen table.

Frank was all alone in the world.

Eugenia Lincoln was right, of course. He was going to have to return to Buddy Lamp's Used Goods.

He was going to have to face his fears.

He was going to have to step forward bravely.

The next day, Frank went to Buddy Lamp's and stared in the window at the weasel and the weasel's teeth and the headless man. And then he pulled open the door and the sleigh bells rang their merry ring, and Frank went inside.

It was, if possible, even gloomier in Buddy Lamp's Used Goods than it had been the day before. The wax figure of Napoleon was gone, and in its place was a gigantic book on a wooden stand. The book was opened to a map. Frank stepped closer. He leaned in and studied the map. He did not recognize anything on it, and the words describing the unrecognizable place were in a different language. Even the letters looked strange. It was all very disconcerting.

Frank took a step back, away from the book.

"Hello?" he called out. "Mr. Lamp?"

"Mr. Endicott," said Buddy Lamp.

"Eeep!" said Frank.

Buddy Lamp had, again, managed to appear out of nowhere.

"Sir!" said Frank. "When you made the key for Miss Lincoln, you put a third key in the envelope by mistake. I'm returning it."

Frank held out the key. He was embarrassed to see that his hand was trembling.

Buddy Lamp bent over. He lowered his glasses. He stared at the key in Frank's shaking hand. "Hmmm," said Buddy Lamp. "Humdee dum dee." He raised his glasses. He stood up straight. He said, "I've never seen that key before."

"What?" said Frank. "That can't be. This key was in the envelope. You must have put it there."

"But I didn't put it there," said Buddy Lamp. He smiled his ghostly smile.

"How did it get in there then?" said Frank. He felt dizzy. "There has to be an explanation."

"Does there?" said Buddy Lamp. "In my experience, things happen all the time that can't be explained."

"Can you please take this key back?"

"I'm afraid I can't," said Buddy Lamp.

"Why not?" said Frank.

"Because," said Buddy Lamp. He smiled. "It's not my key."

"I don't know what to do," said Frank. "I'm confused and afraid."

"Ah," said Buddy Lamp. "I think I have the solution for that."

"You do?" said Frank.

"Yes," said Buddy Lamp.

"What is it?"

"Hot chocolate," said Buddy Lamp.

Chapter Six

Buddy Lamp made hot chocolate by first heating milk on a little two-burner stove. Why, Frank wondered, did people believe so ardently in the heating up of milk? Why did they think it was a solution for anything?

Buddy Lamp's stove was on a table behind the counter, and on either side of the table were pink chairs. Both chairs had stuffing poking out of them.

"Please," said Buddy Lamp. "Have a seat."

Frank sat down. He still had hold of the third key.

"Now," said Buddy Lamp. "I will just heat this milk to the proper temperature and melt the chocolate into it and it will be sweet and good. Then we can drink it together and talk of things that matter."

"Like where this key came from?" said Frank.

"Ha-ha-ha and humdee dum dee," said Buddy Lamp. He dropped chunks of chocolate into the milk. "The key is a mystery. You have been given the gift of a mystery. Isn't that wonderful? Who knows what doors it may unlock? It's like a story from our friend O. Henry."

As far as Frank knew, he didn't have a friend named O. Henry.

Also, he didn't think that mysteries were gifts at all.

Buddy Lamp carefully poured the hot chocolate into two china teacups. He handed a cup to Frank, and then he sank down in his chair and crossed his left leg over his right leg. He took a sip of his hot chocolate. He sighed.

Frank put the key on the table between them.

Outside, from far away, came the sound of thunder. And then there was rain, pattering on the roof of Buddy Lamp's Used Goods.

"Who's O. Henry?" said Frank.

"Tsk," said Buddy Lamp. He put down his teacup. He slowly unfolded himself, got up out of the chair, and disappeared into the confines of the store. When he returned, he had a book in his hands.

He handed the book to Frank and sat down again.

"A Collection of Short Stories Certain to Entertain, Inspire, and Delight," Frank read aloud.

"You'll find a story by O. Henry in there," said Buddy Lamp. "O. Henry is a fabricated name, a pen name, a nom de plume. You can do that, you know: name yourself whatever you please, even if you're not a writer. Take, for example, the name Buddy Lamp. My father was named Buddy

Lamp, and his father before him. But it's a fabricated name, entirely fabricated, born of longing."

"Oh," said Frank.

"Yes," said Buddy Lamp. "It's an interesting story, how the name Buddy Lamp came about. Would you like to hear it?"

"I guess so," said Frank. "And then maybe you can tell me where the third key came from."

"So," said Buddy Lamp, "my grandfather came to this country from Italy. He came on his own. He was only fifteen years old. And when he got off the boat and had to announce his name to the authorities, my grandfather thought, *I am entirely alone in the world. I can become whoever I want to become. I can name myself whatever name I choose.* He said to the man standing next to him in line, 'I would like a name full of light.' And the man beside him said, 'Yeah? Well, turn yourself into a lamp then, buddy.' So that is what my grandfather did. He turned himself into Buddy Lamp."

"That's a good story," said Frank. He took a sip of hot chocolate. He looked over at the third key.

"Good stories help," said Buddy Lamp, "don't they?"

"With what?" said Frank.

"With everything," said Buddy Lamp. "When I was a boy and I couldn't sleep, when the world seemed blustery and unbearably sad, my father would make hot chocolate for me. And then he would sit beside me and read me a story. Are you unbearably sad?"

"I think I'm unbearably worried," said Frank.

"Well," said Buddy Lamp, "stories are good for that, too."

"I'm not much for stories," said Frank. "I prefer a factual account of things. I like to know as many facts as possible."

"Yes," said Buddy Lamp. "I see. Well, stories are factual accounts of the human heart. If you hand me that volume, I will demonstrate."

Frank gave Buddy Lamp the book. He watched him flip through the pages until he came to a story called "The Last Leaf" by O. Henry.

"And so," said Buddy Lamp. He adjusted his glasses. He cleared his throat, and then he read Frank a story about two artists who shared an apartment. The artists were poor and it was winter and one of them got very sick, and she decided that she would die as

soon as the last leaf fell from a vine outside the window of their apartment. But something surprising happened: the last leaf never fell. No matter how hard the wind blew, the last leaf did not fall. It never fell. And the artist did not die.

Frank sat in the pink chair and held his hot chocolate and listened to Buddy

Lamp read. He forgot about the third key and the book of worries and unsolvable mysteries.

"So," said Buddy Lamp when he had finished reading. "You see how things go in stories—how they can surprise you, how things happen that you do not at all anticipate. Maybe that is how it is with

your key. Maybe something will happen that you do not expect at all."

Buddy Lamp closed the book and handed it to Frank.

"Take that with you," he said. "Share its contents with someone else. Make a little light." He stood and gave a little bow and then turned toward the window. "I see that it's raining outside. I have an umbrella that you can borrow. And please, do not leave without your mysterious key."

Chapter Seven

Frank left Buddy Lamp's with *A Collection of Short Stories Certain to Entertain, Inspire, and Delight* under his arm, the third key in his pocket, and an umbrella over his head. The umbrella had a vulture carved into its handle, and normally Frank would not have wanted to carry a vulture umbrella (vultures were very disturbing birds), but he was distracted.

The whole way home, Frank thought about the O. Henry story. He thought about the last leaf and why it was that it never fell. He thought about all the ways that people can surprise each other. He felt warm inside. It was probably the hot chocolate, but maybe it was the story, too.

"Humdee dum dee," said Frank out loud. And then he said it again, "Humdee dum dee."

When Frank got home, he found Stella's friend Horace Broom sitting at the kitchen table with Stella. They were working together on constructing a model of the solar system. They were arguing about what color to paint the planets.

Mercy Watson was under the kitchen table. She had her chin on Stella's foot. She was asleep, and snoring.

"I think that Jupiter should be green," said Stella.

"But it's not green!" said Horace. "Jupiter is not a green planet."

"I didn't say that it was," said Stella. "I'm just saying that I think it would look very good green. It would kind of make the whole solar system look better, zippier."

"We're not making art; we're making the solar system," said Horace Broom. "And we have to do it right."

Stella looked up at Frank. She said, "Where you have you been, Frank?"

Frank said, "I was at a place called Buddy Lamp's Used Goods. I went with Miss Lincoln to get a key duplicated, and when Mr. Lamp gave me the key and its duplicate back, there was a third key in the envelope. This key." He took the key out of his pocket and held it out so that Stella and Horace could see it. "But Mr. Lamp says he did not put this key in the envelope. He says he's never seen it before. It's a mystery."

"Oooh," said Stella. "What if the key opens a treasure chest? And what if the treasure chest is full of gold doubloons?"

“There aren’t doubloons anymore,” said Horace. “All the doubloons have been discovered.”

“How do you know they’ve all been discovered?” said Stella.

“I think that the key opens the door to a prison where someone has been locked away for years and years,” said Horace Broom. He scratched his head. “I think that this is the key that frees someone.”

The three of them studied the key in Frank’s hand.

Mercy Watson woke up. She came to stand with them. She stared at the key, too. She narrowed her eyes.

“Mercy thinks it’s something to eat,” said Stella.

“Ha,” said Horace Broom. “Pigs.”

Mercy leaned forward and snuffled the key. Her snout tickled Frank's fingers. He laughed.

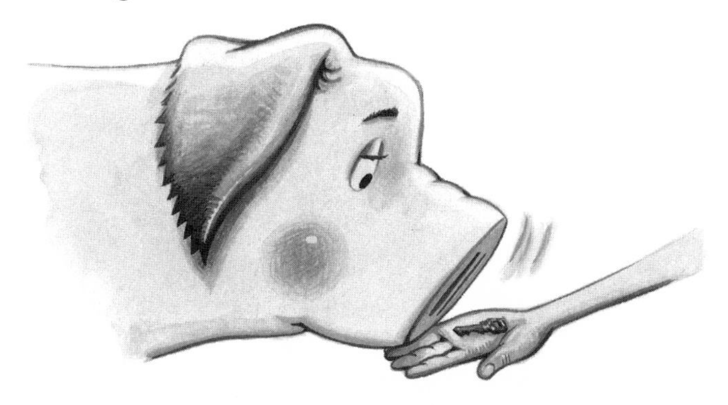

And then, without any warning at all, Mercy Watson sucked up the key and swallowed it.

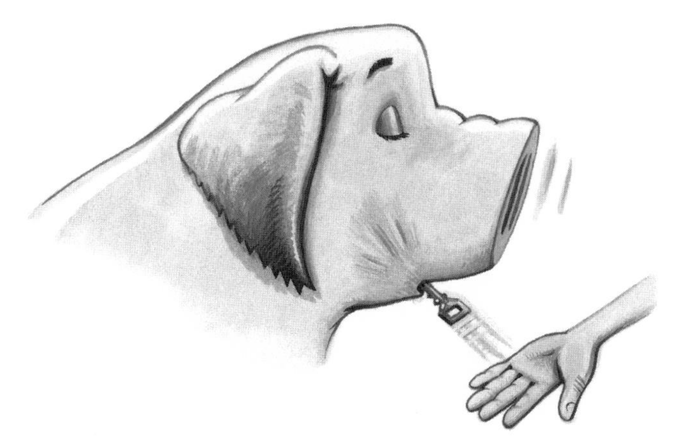

"She ate the key!" shouted Frank. "Mercy ate the key!"

“Do the Heimlich maneuver!” Horace shouted back.

“Why?” said Stella. “She’s not choking.”

And it was true. The pig was not choking. She was standing and staring off into the distance with a benign, if somewhat disappointed, look on her face.

"Well," said Horace. "I guess that takes care of the key mystery."

"Good grief," said Frank. "What if it kills her?"

"She's fine," said Stella. "She can eat anything."

"Pigs have got great digestive tracts," said Horace Broom.

"Good grief," said Frank again.

The warm feeling, the peaceful feeling, the humdee-dum-dee feeling that he had experienced on his walk home from Buddy Lamp's Used Goods, had disappeared entirely. In its place was a familiar sense of dread.

Frank went and got his worry notebook out of the hall closet. He went up to his room and sat down at his desk. He opened the notebook, and then he realized he didn't even know where to start. Should he write down mysterious keys as a worry? Should he list pigs swallowing keys as a concern?

He closed the notebook. He felt a sudden, desperate need to consult the Bingham

Lincoln Encyclopedia set. He went downstairs.

He heard Horace Broom say, "Fine. Paint Jupiter green."

He heard Stella say, "I think you've made an excellent decision. It will look very zippy."

He heard Mercy Watson burp.

Frank went out the door and across the rain-spangled lawn. The sun was coming out. He knocked on the Lincoln sisters' door, and Eugenia Lincoln welcomed him inside. She afforded him carte blanche with the encyclopedias and told him to put everything back where he found it. Frank went and sat in the living room and stared at the books.

He truly didn't know where to begin.

Should he look under *key*?

Mystery?

Digestive tract?

Humdee dum dee?

After a while, Frank got up and went home, without having removed a single Bingham Lincoln Encyclopedia from the shelf.

Chapter Eight

That night, Frank had nightmares. He dreamed about Mercy Watson coughing up eyeballs. He dreamed of a vulture flying over his head, following him. He dreamed that he was looking for something and could not find it. It was exhausting—to look for something and never find it.

When he woke up, he went downstairs and warmed up some milk—although he was beginning to doubt the efficacy of warm milk, and of hot chocolate, too.

Truthfully, he was starting to doubt everything. It was a terrible feeling.

He saw that the Lincolns' kitchen light was on. Eugenia Lincoln was sitting at the kitchen table. She looked lonely and unbearably sad.

Frank went upstairs and retrieved *A Collection of Short Stories Certain to Entertain, Inspire, and Delight.* He wrote another note to his family (*Do not worry. I have just gone next door. Love, Frank*) and then he took two mugs of warm milk, walked over to the Lincoln sisters' house, and called out, "It's me, Miss Lincoln. Franklin Endicott. Could you open the door? I've got my hands rather full here."

Eugenia Lincoln opened the door.

Frank said, "I made you some hot milk with cinnamon and honey, Miss Lincoln. And I thought you might want to know that I took the key back to Mr. Lamp and he said that it wasn't his, that he had never seen it before, and that he didn't know how it had gotten into the envelope. He says that it's a mystery. And that mysteries are gifts."

Eugenia snorted.

"I don't know that I agree with him," said Frank. "But in any case, I suppose it doesn't matter, because now the key is gone entirely."

"Gone where?" said Eugenia. She led Frank to the kitchen.

"I don't think you want to know," said Frank. "It involves Mercy Watson."

Eugenia snorted again. "Of course it involves that pig—that insufferable, insufferable pig."

"In any case," said Frank, "when I went to try and return the key to Mr. Lamp, he made me hot chocolate and read me a story, and it was very comforting. I thought that I might read you a story, too. I thought it might calm us both down."

"I'm perfectly calm," said Eugenia. She tapped her fingers on the table.

"Okay," said Frank. "Anyway. Let's see here." He opened the book to a story entitled "The Door in the Wall" by someone named H. G. Wells.

"'One confidential evening,'" read Frank aloud. And he and Eugenia settled together into a magical story about a green

door that opened onto a beautiful garden and how this door in the wall had haunted a man for his whole life, ever since he had walked through it as a child.

It was a sad story and a beautiful story. It was a story filled with wonder and mystery. Frank read and read. His voice was unwavering. He was good at reading out loud, and when he read the last word of "The Door in the Wall," Eugenia Lincoln was silent for a long time.

"Hmmmphh," she said at last. "You may read another, I suppose."

Frank thought how mysterious the world was, how unexplainable and sometimes frightening. But to sit in the kitchen and read to someone he loved and to push back the darkness with a story—that was a wonderful thing.

"Okay," he said. He flipped through the collection of stories until he came to one by Langston Hughes entitled "Thank You, Ma'am." The story began with a very funny sentence: "She was a large woman with a large purse that had everything in it but hammer and nails."

The woman with the large purse was named Mrs. Luella Bates Washington Jones, and in the story she invited home someone who had tried to rob her. She sat the robber down in her kitchen and fed him. She made him cocoa.

Just like Buddy Lamp! thought Frank.

When Frank finished reading the story, Eugenia Lincoln said, "I would not tolerate anyone stealing my purse, I can tell you that much." She smiled a small smile.

"But I have to say that I admire Mrs. Luella Bates Washington Jones. She is someone I would very much like to meet."

"Me too," said Frank. "I would like to sit at her table."

He yawned. He closed the book of stories. It made a solid, certain thump.

"Good night, Miss Lincoln," he said.

"Good night, Franklin Endicott," said Eugenia.

⁂

Frank slept.

He dreamed of standing in front of a green door.

He knocked on the door, but no one answered.

And then he looked down at his hand and realized that he had the key. *Oh,* he thought, *this is what the third key is for. It unlocks the green door.*

He put the key in the lock and it worked. The door swung wide, and Frank was suddenly in a room filled with light.

He stood in the room and held the key in his hand, and he was happier than he had ever been.

Somewhere, someone was playing an accordion.

Frank sang along. "Humdee dum dee," he sang. "Humdee dum dee."

When he woke up, the sun was shining. He could still hear accordion music, and the room was filled with light just as it had been in his dream.

Frank got out of bed and went to the window. He looked out and saw Eugenia Lincoln in her backyard. She was playing the accordion. She was smiling.

Frank went to visit Buddy Lamp.

He took his book of worries. He said, "I wonder if I could leave this here with you."

"Certainly," said Buddy Lamp. He flipped through the notebook. "Hmmm," he said, "what a comprehensive list. It's very detailed. Very thorough."

"Yes, well," said Frank.

"You know that if you look at these things differently, from a slightly different angle, you could see them not as worries, but as marvels—things to be amazed by.

The speed of alligators! The mystery of black holes! Humdee dum dee."

"A pig ate the third key," said Frank.

"A pig?" said Buddy Lamp.

"Yes," said Frank. "A pig."

Buddy Lamp let out a whoop of laughter. He said, "O. Henry would be pleased.

And speaking of Mr. Henry, I see you've brought the book back."

"Yes," said Frank. "I thought I would read you a story."

"Excellent," said Buddy Lamp. He clapped his hands together. "Oh, wonderful. I will make us some hot chocolate."

Coda

It took a while, but Frank made it through the entire volume of entertaining, inspiring, and delightful short stories. He read stories out loud to Buddy Lamp. He read stories to Eugenia Lincoln. He read to Stella and to Horace Broom.

Sometimes, when no one else was around, Frank read to Mercy Watson.

She did a relatively good job of listening.

Frank would look up from his book and see Mercy staring at him and think: *There is a key inside of her. She contains a mystery.* And then he would think: *I guess we all contain mysteries.*

Frank kept a notebook for the rest of his life.

It was not a notebook of worries.

It was a notebook of marvels.

He called the notebook "The Third Key," and he wrote in it under the pen name "H. D. D. Frank."

In the notebook's pages, H. D. D. Frank considered the mysteries.

He celebrated the marvels.

He made some light.

Humdee Dum Dee.

THE
THIRD
KEY
by
H.D.D. FRANK